DC COMICS™

BATMAN™

TALES OF THE BATCAVE

BATCAVE

THE CRUSHING COIN

by
MICHAEL DAHL

illustrated by

LUCIANO VECCHIO

Batman created by
BOB KANE WITH BILL FINGER

Raintree is an imprint of Capstone Global Library Limited, a
company incorporated in England and Wales having its
registered office at 264 Banbury Road, Oxford, OX2 7DY –
Registered company number: 6695582

www.raintree.co.uk
myorders@raintree.co.uk

Text © Capstone Global Library Limited 2017
The moral rights of the proprietor have been asserted.

ISBN 978 1 4747 2912 3
20 19 18 17 16
10 9 8 7 6 5 4 3 2 1

British Library Cataloguing in Publication Data
A full catalogue record for this book is available from the British Library.

Every effort has been made to contact copyright holders of material reproduced in this
book. Any omissions will be rectified in subsequent printings if notice is given to the
publisher.

All the internet addresses (URLs) given in this book were valid at the time of going to
press. However, due to the dynamic nature of the internet, some addresses may have
changed, or sites may have changed or ceased to exist since publication. While the
author and publisher regret any inconvenience this may cause readers, no responsibility
for any such changes can be accepted by either the author or the publisher.

Editor: Christopher Harbo
Designer: Bob Lentz
Production Specialist: Kathy McColley

Printed and bound in China.

CONTENTS

This is the BATCAVE.

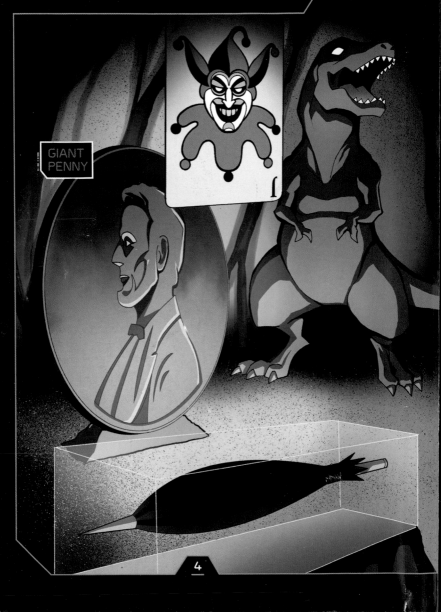

GIANT PENNY

It is the secret headquarters of
Batman and his crime-fighting
partner, Robin.

Hundreds of trophies, awards and
souvenirs fill the Batcave's hidden
rooms. Each one tells a story of
danger, villainy and victory.

This is the tale of a giant penny!
And why this trophy now stands
in the Batcave . . .

CHAPTER 1

DOUBLE WHAMMY

A fierce-looking motorcycle squeals to a stop in a dark side street.

Robin, the Boy Wonder, speaks into a microphone on his collar.

"I got here in double-quick time, Batman," he says. "But something feels wrong."

The Batcycle is parked near the back doors
of the Eagle Eyeglasses Company.

Robin looks up and down the street. There's
no one in sight.

"It's too quiet for a robbery to be happening," says Robin.

"It's quiet here, too," says a powerful voice in Robin's earphones.

"But Commissioner Gordon got tip-offs that Eagle Eyeglasses and Gotham Boot would be robbed tonight," Batman continues.

"Two tip-offs for two robberies at two ends of town!" says Robin. "Sounds like the work of Two-Face."

"This latest crime wave only hits places that sell things in pairs," Batman says. "I'm sure that double-dealing crook is behind it!"

"But he hits two places each night," says Robin. "At the exact same time."

"Exactly. And Two-Face usually works alone," adds Batman. "So how does he do it?"

Two alarm bells ring.

One blares directly over Robin's head.
The other crackles from his earphones.

"He's hit again!" comes Batman's voice.
"Another double whammy!"

CHAPTER 2

WHOSE FACE?

A security guard runs down the side street.

"Boy Wonder!" yells the guard. "There's a scary-looking guy inside the building!"

"Two-Face!" mumbles Robin.

"This way!" says the guard, motioning to a door.

"I'll go in first," says Robin. "Don't let his face freak you out."

The guard stands behind Robin as the Boy Wonder enters the door.

The guard's face begins to melt. His uniform slowly dissolves.

He grows in size and shape, until he looks like a walking hunk of clay.

The creature lunges towards the Boy Wonder.

His fist falls like an avalanche of mud. The blow knocks Robin out.

The creature lifts the young hero in his dripping arms.

"I'm the face you need to fear, kid," he says. "Clayface!"

CHAPTER 3

GETTING THE BOOT!

On the other side of town, Batman's ejector seat shoots him up and out of the Batmobile.

The Dark Knight swoops through an open window in the Gotham Boot factory.

"What took you so long, Caped Crusader?" comes a snarl from across a large room.

"Two-Face!" the Dark Knight says.

"You knew I'd be here, didn't you?" says the villain.

Batman pulls a coin from his Utility Belt.

"I've been finding these coins at the crime scenes all week," he says.

"So it's as plain as the nose on my face?" hoots Two-Face.

"It's even plainer that you're going back to prison," says Batman.

"I don't do prison anymore," Two-Face replies as he pushes a button on a remote control. "I've kicked that habit."

Two small explosions burst apart a set of chains holding up a gigantic boot on display.

Swiftly, Batman leaps to safety. The giant boot hits the floor with a mighty thud!

"I'm one step ahead of you," says Batman.

"Not so fast," the villain cries. "All good things come in pairs!"

BOOM! BOOM!

A second giant boot falls from the shadows.

Batman is knocked unconscious. He lies under the huge heel of the boot.

Two-Face stands over him and laughs.

"Looks like the other shoe has dropped!"
the villain says.

CHAPTER 4

THE OTHER SIDE OF THE COIN

"Batman!" shouts Robin. "Where are you?"

Batman wakes up. His body is now upright.

Batman sees metal bars around his waist and wrists. He is bound to a gigantic coin.

"Robin!" Batman calls.

"I'm here, Batman," yells the Boy Wonder. "On the other side of this overgrown penny!"

"Two faces on the same coin!" says Two-Face with glee.

"But only one face survives!" adds Clayface.

The villains stand on the floor, looking up at their prisoners. Two-Face holds on to the edge of the heavy coin.

"You usually work alone!" Robin says.

"I've rarely found anyone with a face I trust," says Two-Face. "Until now, that is."

Clayface laughs. His face morphs into a copy of Two-Face's.

"The two faces of Two-Face!" says Robin.

"We committed our robberies at the same times so you'd split up to come after us," says Clayface. "Divide and conquer!"

"Time for the game to start!" says Two-Face. "Let's flip the coin."

"After this spins, only one of you will land face up," the villain continues. "The other will be crushed by two tonnes of copper!"

Clayface shouts, "No more Dynamic Duo!"

CHAPTER 5

END OF THE WHIRLED

The massive coin spins and spins.

"What do we do?" cries Robin. "I can't think! My head is spinning!"

"My legs are free," says Batman. "Are yours?"

"Yeah, I'm just held by this metal belt," answers the Boy Wonder. "How do we escape?"

"Physics, Robin! Physics!" calls out the Dark Knight. "Swing your legs to create enough force to keep the coin spinning!"

The heroes pump their legs out and in on each side of the coin.

"It's working, Batman!" shouts Robin. "Just like a swing on a playground!"

Two-Face stares and does a double-take.

"This can't be happening!" he cries.

"You fool!" says Clayface. "No wonder
nobody wants to work with you!"

The mucky monster turns to flee.

Batman's special glove helps him squeeze his hand out of his wrist restraint. He reaches for a button on his Utility Belt.

A Batarang shoots out towards the two villains. The circling weapon wraps a wire around Two-Face and Clayface.

As the coin spins, the wire drags the villains around the room.

YAAAAIIEEEEEEEEEHHHH!

Batman presses another button on his belt.

A stream of plastic goo spurts out of the belt. It hits the floor and hardens, stopping the spinning coin.

It also traps the dizzy evil pair.

The heroes use lasers from their belts to cut through their restraints.

Batman grins at the two villains.

"Your big mistake was bringing us back
together," says the Dark Knight. "Two heads
are always better than one."

"These crooks never learn," says Robin.
"They should know crime never pays!"

"A penny for your thoughts, Batman."

"Hmm, do you think this coin will fit inside the Batcave, Robin?"

"Sure, we could float it through the underground river."

"So we use the cash flow method?"

"Funny, Batman. Very funny."

Glossary

avalanche mass of snow, rocks, ice or soil that slides down a mountain slope

conquer defeat and take control of an enemy

dissolve disappear into something else

double whammy combination of two blows or setbacks

morph change in shape

physics study of matter and energy, including light, heat, electricity and motion

restraint something that limits movement

tonne a unit of weight equal to 1000 kilograms

unconscious not awake; not able to see, feel or think

Discuss

1. Two-Face rarely teams up with other villains. Why do you think he chose Clayface to be his partner?

2. Batman already knew Two-Face was behind the crime wave before the story started. What two clues helped him figure it out?

3. Who was the more dangerous villain? Why?

Write

1. The Dynamic Duo used the science of motion to keep the coin from slowing down and falling on one of them. Was there another way they could have escaped?

2. Two-Face likes to rob places that have something to do with pairs. Make a list other shops the crook might have robbed before this story began.

3. Clayface's superpower allows him to change his shape. If you could change into anything, what would you choose and why?

Author

Michael Dahl is the prolific author of the best-selling *Goodnight Baseball* picture book and more than 200 other books for children and young adults. In the United States, he has won the AEP Distinguished Achievement Award three times for his non-fiction, a Teachers' Choice Award from *Learning* magazine, and a Seal of Excellence from the Creative Child Awards. He is also the author of the Hocus Pocus Hotel mystery series and the Dragonblood books. Dahl currently lives in Minneapolis, Minnesota, USA.

Illustrator

Luciano Vecchio was born in 1982 and is based in Buenos Aires, Argentina. Freelance artist for many projects at Marvel and DC Comics, his work has been seen in print and online around the world. He has illustrated many DC Super Heroes books for Capstone, and some of his recent comic work includes *Beware the Batman*, *Green Lantern: The Animated Series*, *Young Justice*, *Ultimate Spider-Man,* and his creator-owned web-comic, *Sereno*.